A Day With

GREAT INVENTORS

A Day With

GREAT INVENTORS

MOONSTONE

Published in Moonstone
by Rupa Publications India Pvt. Ltd 2023
7/16, Ansari Road, Daryaganj
New Delhi 110002

Sales centres:
Prayagraj Bengaluru Chennai
Hyderabad Jaipur Kathmandu
Kolkata Mumbai

P-ISBN: 978-93-5520-934-4
E-ISBN: 978-93-5520-935-1

First impression 2023

10 9 8 7 6 5 4 3 2 1

Printed in India

Contents

Alexander Graham Bell

Guglielmo Marconi

Wright Brothers

James Watt

Alexander Graham Bell

Alexander Graham Bell invented the telephone.
What did he do before he invented the telephone?
Read on to discover the answer.

Meet Tim and Tyra

Hi, I'm Tim.

Hi, I'm Tyra. We are going to travel back in time to visit Alexander Graham Bell. Let's meet him now.

Chapter 1: In Alexander Graham Bell's House

Alexander Graham Bell was born on 3 March, 1847 in Edinburgh, **Scotland**.
He was a great **scientist** and **inventor**.

Alexander Graham Bell's mother was **deaf**. She could not hear. Young Bell wanted to find a good way to talk to his mother.

He wanted to learn about sound. He learned how the tongue, lips and throat make sounds.

Alexander Graham Bell learned that sound has
vibrations.
Deaf people can feel vibrations.
Bell thought he could use vibrations to talk to his mother.
Bell talked in a low voice close to his mother's head.
It worked. She could feel the vibrations and she could
understand what Bell said.

Alexander Graham Bell listened to people and animals make sounds.
Bell wanted to see if his dog could make speaking sounds.
He tried moving his dog's mouth.
He pressed his dog's mouth as it growled.
It sounded as if the dog was talking!

When Alexander Graham Bell was 24, he moved to the United States of America.

He became a teacher at a school for the deaf in **Boston**.

There he taught deaf people to speak.

He taught them how to use their throats to make sounds.

He taught them how to move their tongues and lips to turn the sounds into words.

Chapter 6: The Telephone

In the 1870s, there were no telephones.
Alexander Graham Bell wanted to send a person's voice from one place to another.
He invented an object with wires, a **mouthpiece**, a **receiver** and other things.

On 7 March, 1876, Bell was ready to try out his invention.
His helper, Mr Watson, went into another room, where the receiver was. Bell spoke into the mouthpiece. "Mr Watson, come here!" he yelled. Mr Watson heard the shout through the receiver.
So, Bell had invented the telephone!

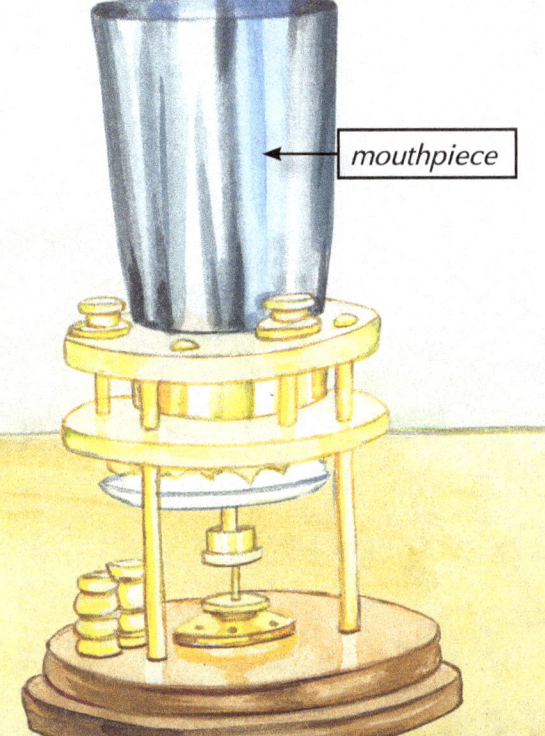

mouthpiece

In 1877, Alexander Graham Bell started his own company.
He called it the Bell Telephone Company.
Soon, there were thousands of people using telephones!

Alexander Graham Bell was also interested in flying. He liked to build and fly kites.

He wanted to make a kite that could carry a person.

He worked with some other people to make a very big kite.

The kite was able to carry a person into the air.

This kite helped people to learn more about how things can fly.

Alexander Graham Bell died on 2 August, 1922 in Nova Scotia, Canada.
What **honour** could the country give him?
All phones were turned off for one minute.
It was a great honor for a great man.

Timeline

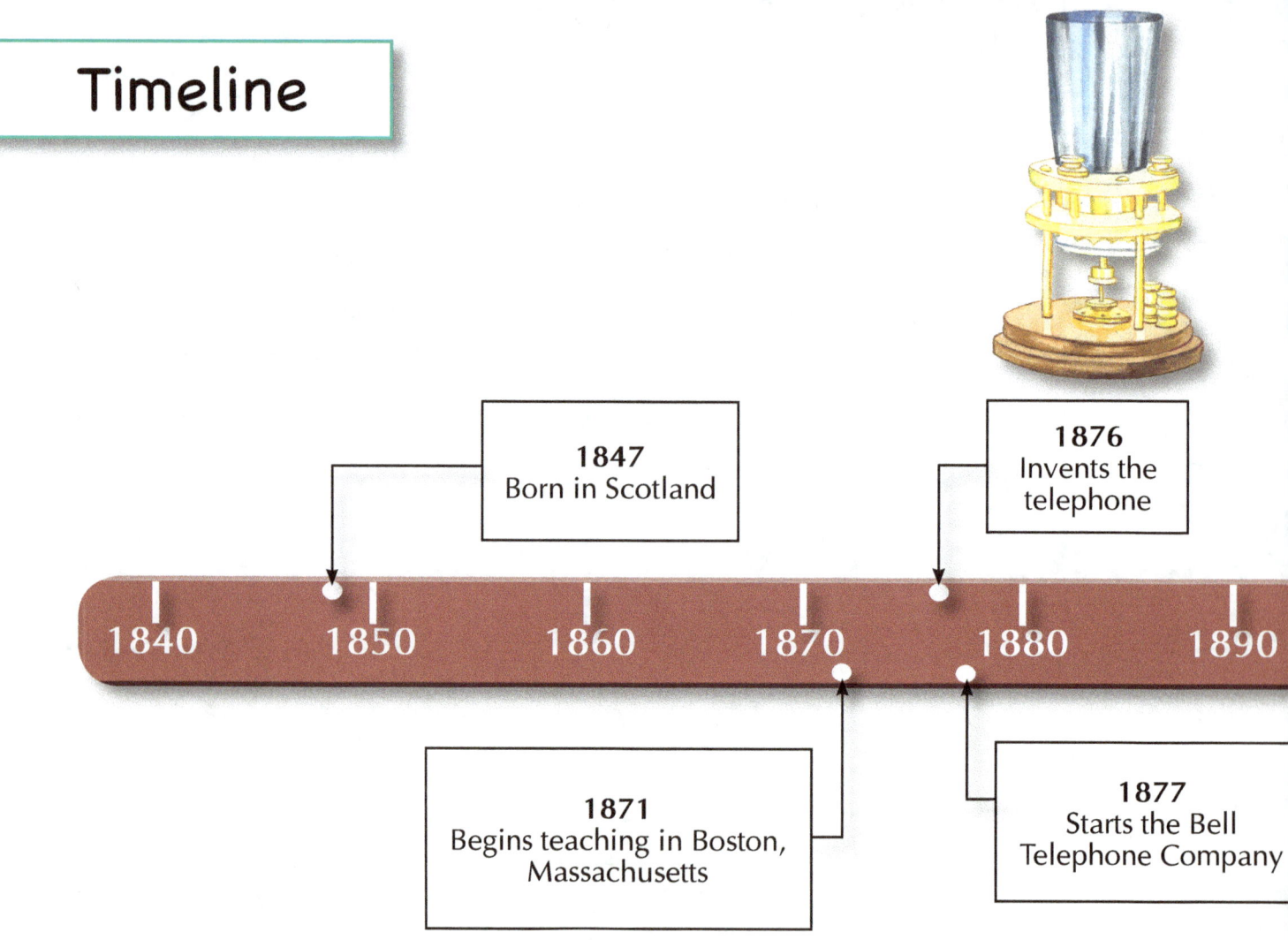

1847
Born in Scotland

1876
Invents the telephone

1840   1850   1860   1870   1880   1890

1871
Begins teaching in Boston, Massachusetts

1877
Starts the Bell Telephone Company

Alexander Graham Bell's Life and Work

1900 | 1910 | 1920 | 1930

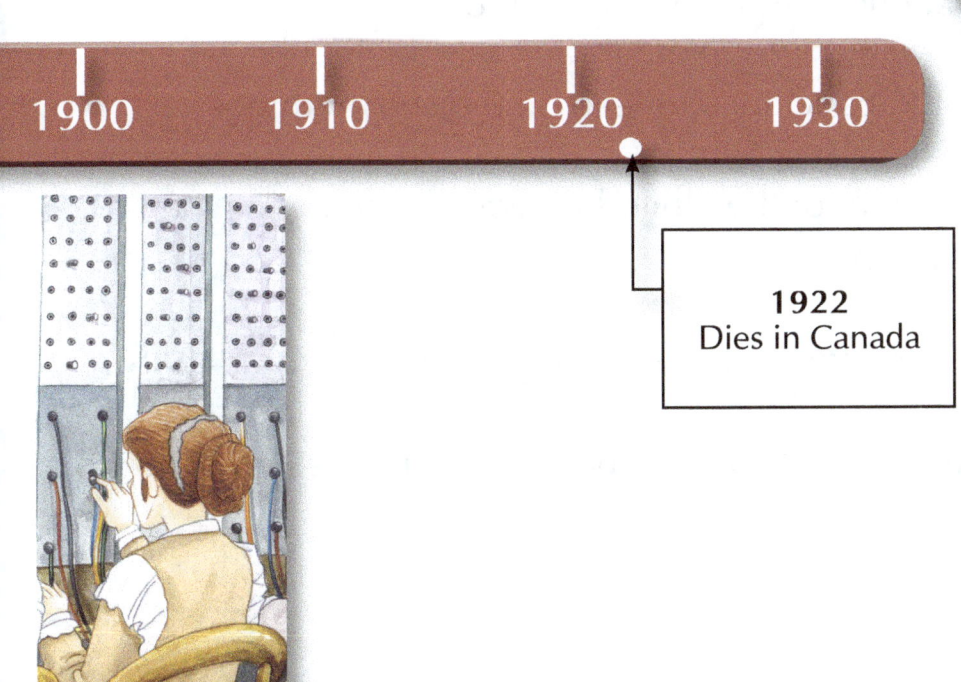

1922
Dies in Canada

Word Meanings

Boston: A city in Massachusetts, a state in north-eastern United States

Deaf: A person who has impaired hearing

Honour: A sign of special respect or admiration

Inventor: A person who makes something new

Mouthpiece: The part of a phone that you speak into

Scientist: A person who studies science to learn and discover things

Scotland: A constituent country of the United Kingdom, occupying the northern part of Great Britain

Receiver: The part of a phone from where sound goes in and comes out

Vibrations: Quick back and forth or up and down movements

Think, Talk and Write

Think About It

On a separate piece of paper, write some of the things Bell did before
he invented the telephone.
Do you think these things helped him invent the telephone?
If so, how? If not, why not?
Write one or two sentences to explain your answer.

Talk About It

Work with a partner who has also read this part of the book.
Pretend you both have a special telephone that lets you talk to Alexander
Graham Bell.
What would you tell him about the times you live in?
Make a list of things you would tell him. Start by telling him three things
about the cell phone.

Write About It

What would life be like without a telephone?
Write a story about how your life would be different if there were no telephones.

What did you learn from Alexander Graham Bell?

What are the five things that you will change after reading Alexander Graham Bell's story?

Guglielmo Marconi

Guglielmo Marconi invented the wireless telegraph.
How did Marconi invent the wireless telegraph?
Read on to discover what he learned.

Meet Tim and Tyra

Hi, I'm Tim.

Hi, I'm Tyra. We are going to travel back in time to visit Marconi. Let's meet him now.

Guglielmo Marconi was born on 25 April, 1874 in Bologna, **Italy**. He was a great **scientist** and **inventor**.

Chapter 2: Boy Scientist

Young Marconi wanted to learn about **radio waves**.
He set up his own **lab**.
The lab was in the attic of his house.
He did many **experiments** there.

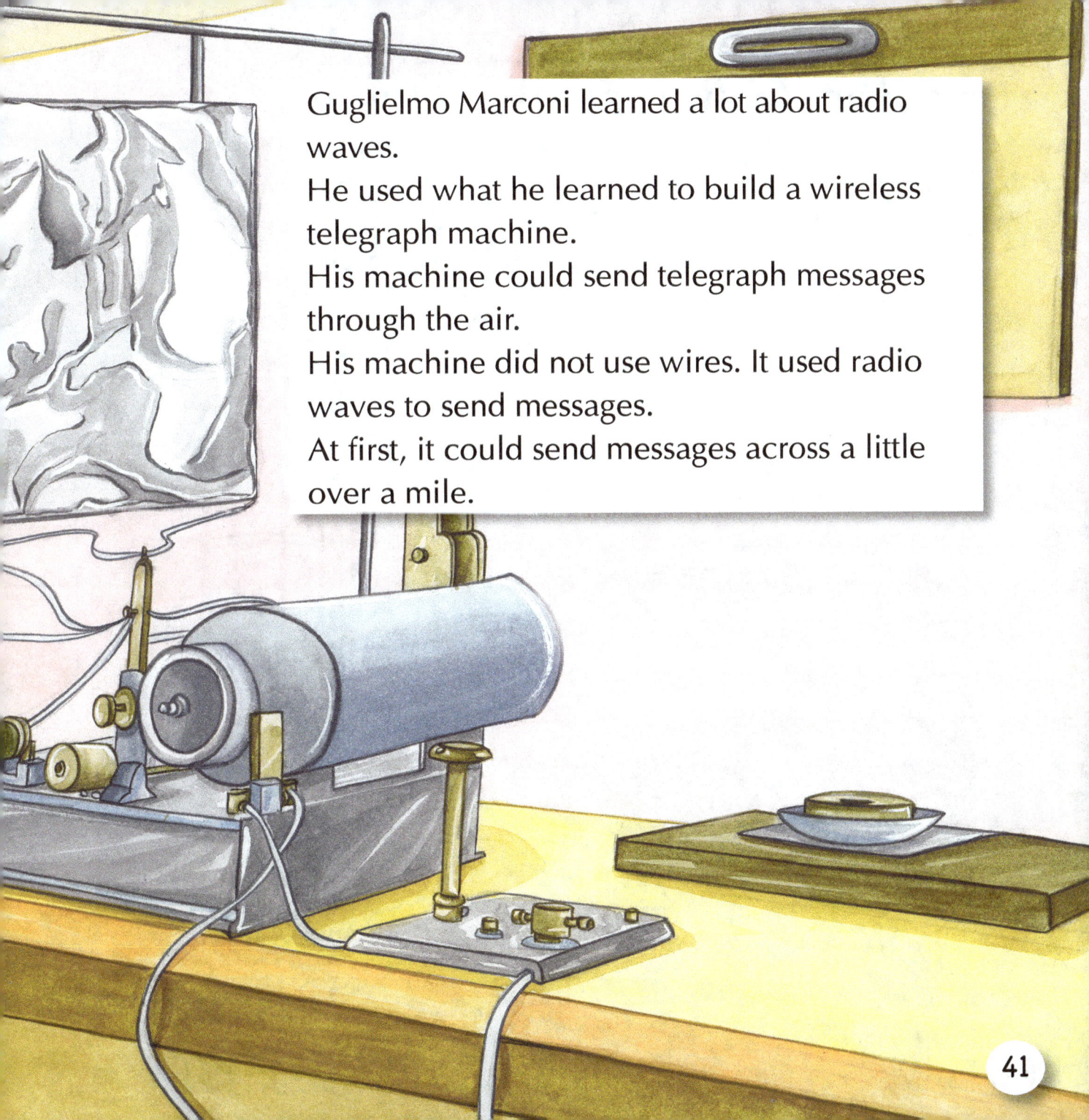

Guglielmo Marconi learned a lot about radio waves.

He used what he learned to build a wireless telegraph machine.

His machine could send telegraph messages through the air.

His machine did not use wires. It used radio waves to send messages.

At first, it could send messages across a little over a mile.

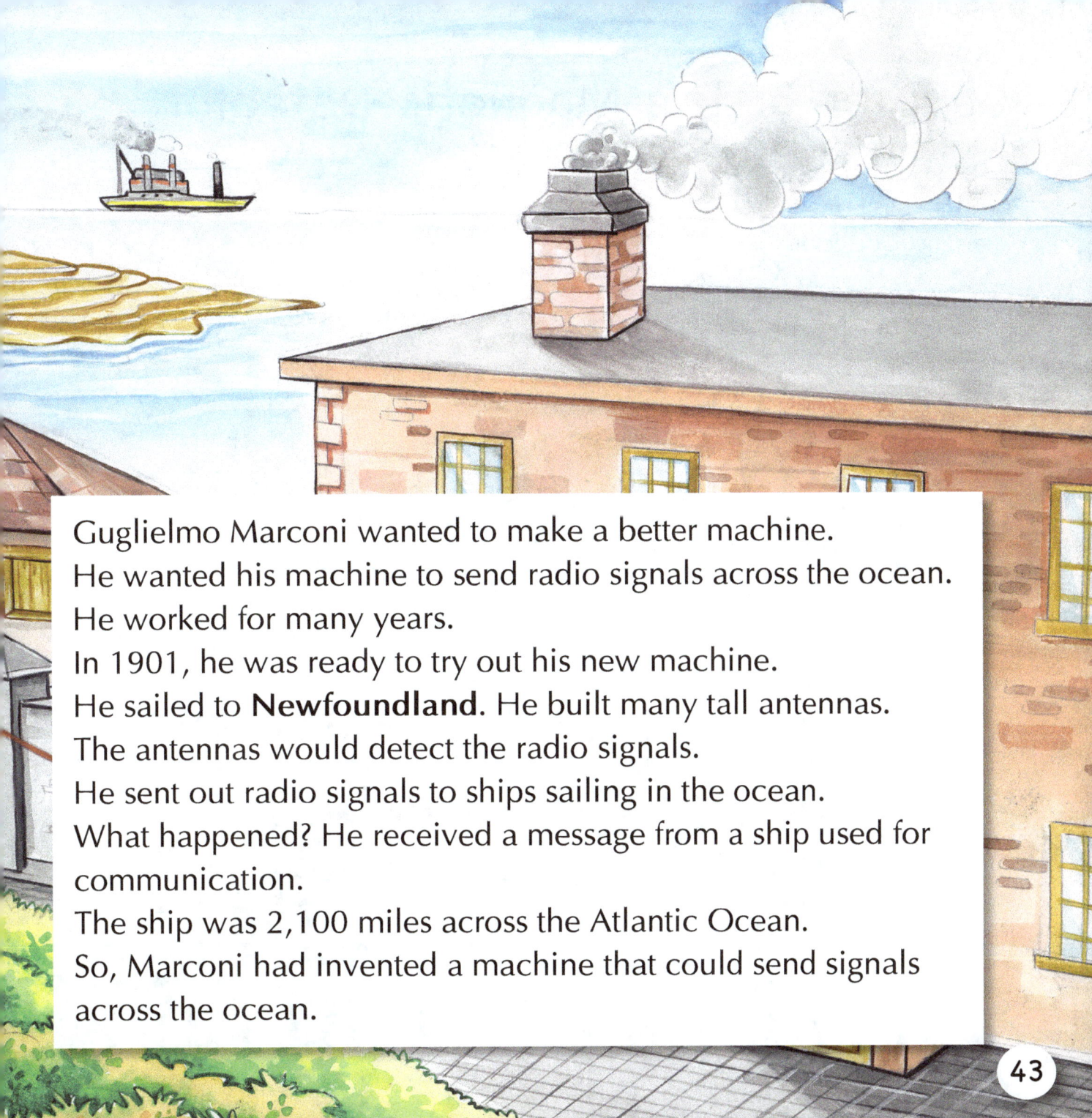

Guglielmo Marconi wanted to make a better machine.
He wanted his machine to send radio signals across the ocean.
He worked for many years.
In 1901, he was ready to try out his new machine.
He sailed to **Newfoundland.** He built many tall antennas.
The antennas would detect the radio signals.
He sent out radio signals to ships sailing in the ocean.
What happened? He received a message from a ship used for communication.
The ship was 2,100 miles across the Atlantic Ocean.
So, Marconi had invented a machine that could send signals across the ocean.

Guglielmo Marconi worked to make his machine even better.
His machine would make dots and dashes on paper.
The dots and dashes made up the message.
Marconi wanted people to listen to these dots and dashes.
What could he do?
He **invented** a new part.
It was called "Maggie" or magnetic detector.
Now, people could hear the signals that he was sending.

Guglielmo Marconi won a big prize in 1909. It was the **Nobel Prize** for Physics.
The Nobel Prize is one of the world's top science awards.
It was a big **honor**.

Guglielmo Marconi's wireless telegraph was fitted in many ships.
It helped ships call for help in times of danger.
The *Titanic* was the largest ship of its time.
It was also fitted with Marconi's wireless telegraph.

The *Titanic* struck an iceberg about 400 miles off the coast of
Newfoundland. The ship sank. Many people died.
But many people were saved too. How?
Marconi's wireless telegraph sent out distress messages.
A ship, that was nearby, came to help.
Marconi's invention helped save the lives of many people.

Guglielmo Marconi invented many useful things.
The radio was one of them.
The radio could send voices over the air.
He set up radio stations and began to broadcast
radio programmes.
It made him very popular.

Guglielmo Marconi died in Rome, Italy on 20 July, 1937.
How could the world honor him?
All radio stations fell silent for two minutes.
It was a great honor for a great man.

Timeline

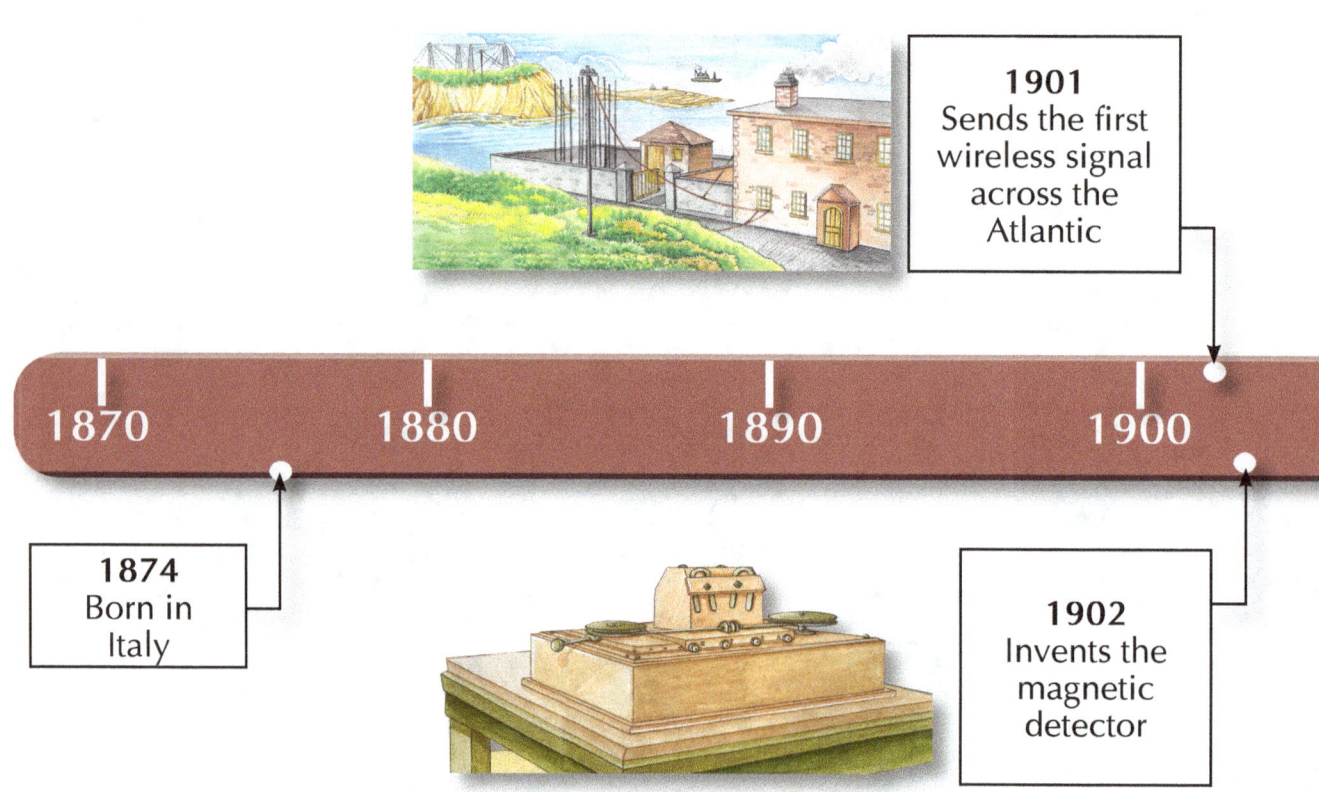

1901
Sends the first wireless signal across the Atlantic

1870   1880   1890   1900

1874
Born in Italy

1902
Invents the magnetic detector

Guglielmo Marconi's Life and Work

1909
Wins the Nobel
Prize for Physics

0   1920   1930   1940

1920
Organizes
Britain's first
public radio
broadcast

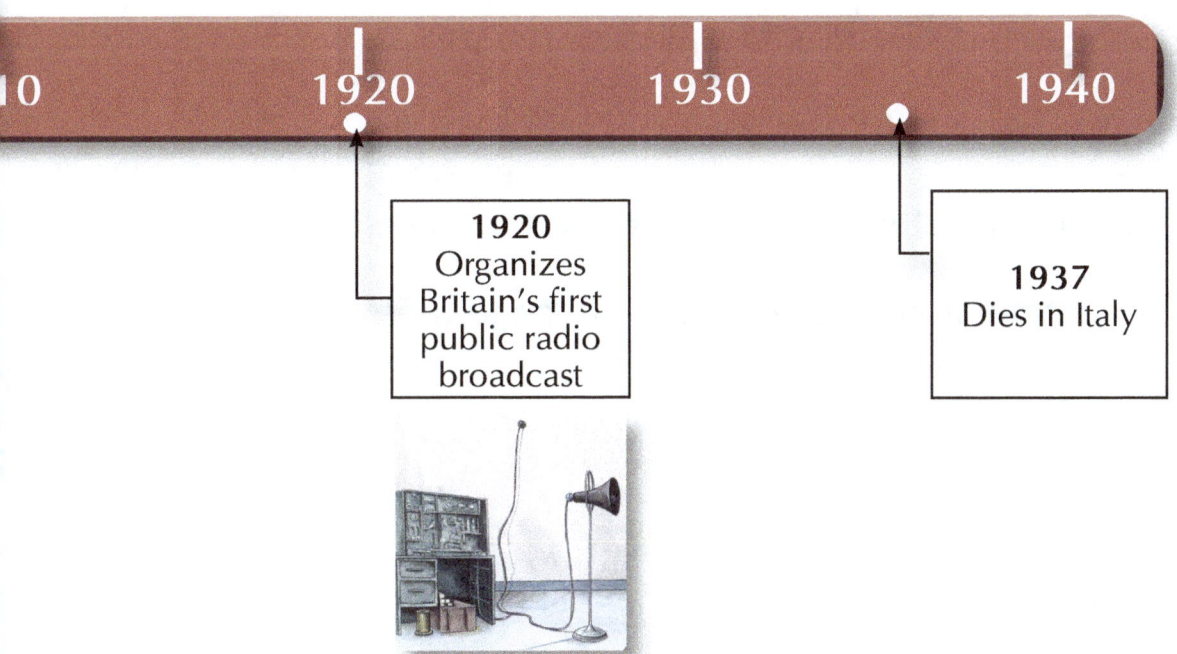

1937
Dies in Italy

Word Meanings

Experiments: Tests to discover something new

Invented: Made something for the first time

Italy: A country in Europe

Lab: A short word for laboratory. A lab is a place to invent or discover new things

Newfoundland: A large island off the north-eastern coast of North America

Nobel Prize: A special prize that honors great work

Radio waves: A form of light that can travel through the air

Scientist: A person who studies science to learn and discover things

Telegraph: A machine that uses electricity to send messages in code

Think, Talk and Write

Think About It

Guglielmo Marconi liked to discover new things.
Think about what you just read.
List three things that use radio waves.

Talk About It

Work with a partner who also read this part of the book.
Pretend you both have a wireless telegraph.
The wireless telegraph lets you send messages to Marconi.
What would you say to Marconi about his invention?

Write About It

What would life be like without the radio?
Write a story about how your life would have been different if there were no radios.

What did you learn from Guglielmo Marconi?

....

....

....

....

....

....

....

....

....

....

....

....

....

....

What are the five things that you will change after reading Guglielmo Marconi's story?

....

....

....

....

....

....

....

....

....

....

....

....

....

....

Orville and Wilbur Wright

Orville and Wilbur Wright invented the airplane.
How did the Wright brothers learn to make airplanes?
Read on to discover the answer.

Meet Tim and Tyra

Hi, I'm Tim.

Hi, I'm Tyra. We are going to travel back in time to visit the Wright Brothers. Let's meet them now.

Wilbur Wright was born on 16 April, 1867 in **Indiana**, USA. His brother Orville was born on 19 August, in **Ohio**, USA. The Wright brothers built the first airplane with a **motor**.

Wilbur and Orville were happy boys.
They loved to read, learn and make things.

One day, their father gave them a toy **helicopter**.
They loved it.
They made their own toy helicopter.
Wilbur was eleven. Orville was only seven.

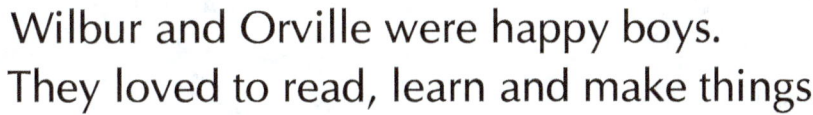

The Wright brothers worked together when they grew up. They were good at fixing things.
They began to fix bicycles.
They began to sell bicycles too.
Then, they started to build their own bicycles.
They found ways to make better bicycles.
A lot of people bought these bicycles.

The brothers wanted to fly too.
How could they fly?
They were good at building things.
What could they build?

69

Chapter 5: Gliders

They could build a glider!
A **glider** is a kind of airplane.
It does not have a motor. It uses wind to fly.
Many people were making gliders back then.
The gliders were hard to **steer**.
The Wright brothers wanted to build a better glider.
They learned more about how birds fly and move their
wings to change directions.

They used what they learned to build a better glider.
Finally, they could steer it well.

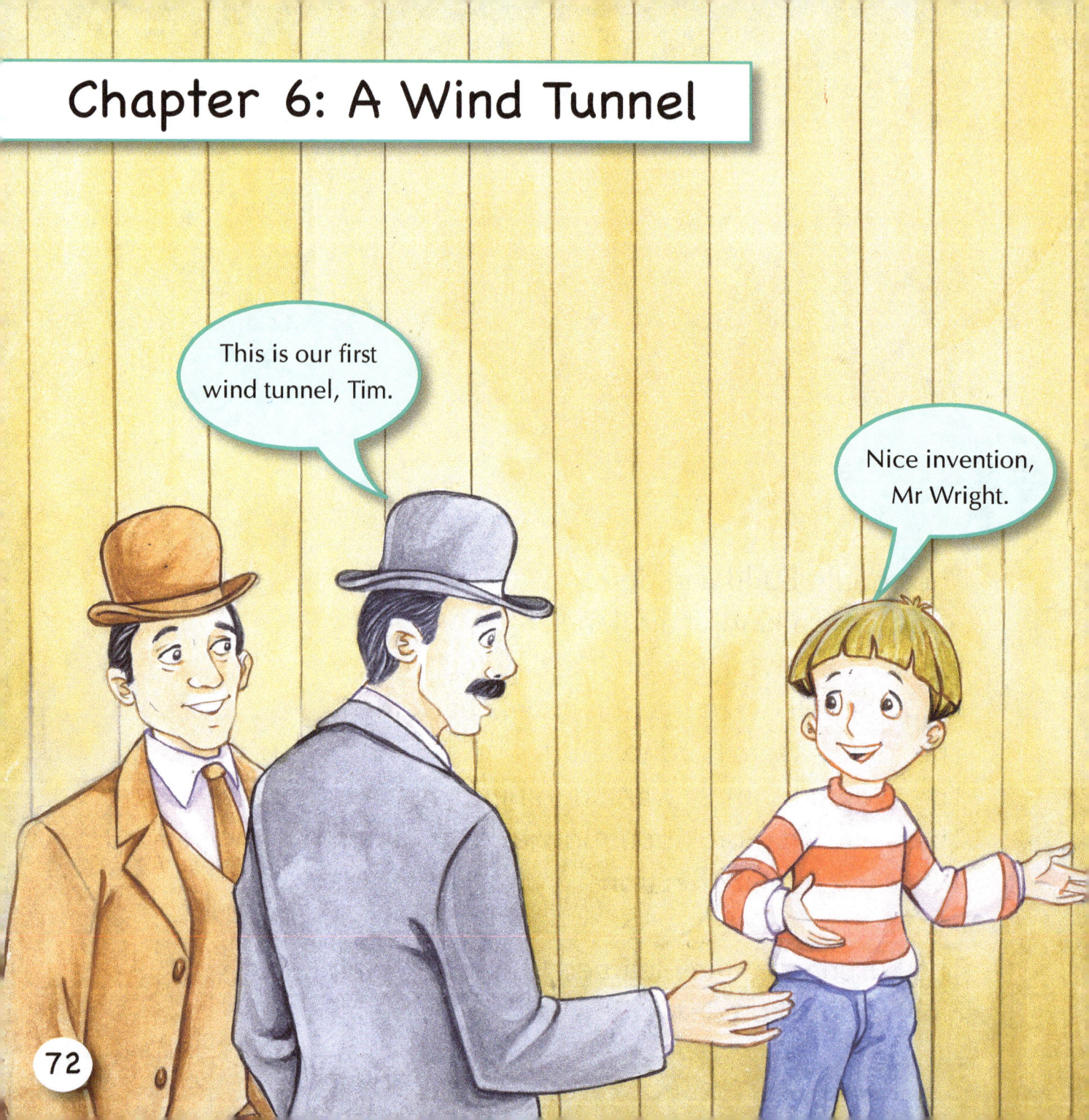

The Wright brothers wanted to learn how wings worked in the wind.
So, they made a **wind tunnel** from a wood box.

They put wings from a **model** airplane in the tunnel.
They attached a fan at the end.
The fan blew wind through the tunnel.
Then, the Wright brothers studied what happened to the wings.

The wind tunnel helped the brothers learn more about flying.

The brothers made a new plane. It had a motor.
They called the plane The Flyer.
They took the plane to a field in **Kitty Hawk**,
North Carolina.
Who would test the plane?
The brothers tossed a coin to decide. Wilbur won.
He got in the plane. It flew for about three seconds.
Then it crashed!

It took three days to fix the plane.
When it was ready, Orville got on the plane.
On 17 December, 1903, the plane flew!
It stayed in the air for twelve seconds.
Then, it safely landed on the ground.
It was a wonderful first flight.

The Wright brothers wanted to build better planes.
They started their own airplane company.
They invented parts for planes.
These parts helped planes fly better.

Wilbur and Orville Wright were great inventors.
They loved to learn new things.
Their flight in Kitty Hawk changed the world.

Wilbur died on 30 May, 1912 in Ohio, USA and
Orville died on 30 January, 1948 in Ohio, USA.

You can see the plane that flew in Kitty Hawk.
It is in a museum in **Washington, D.C.**

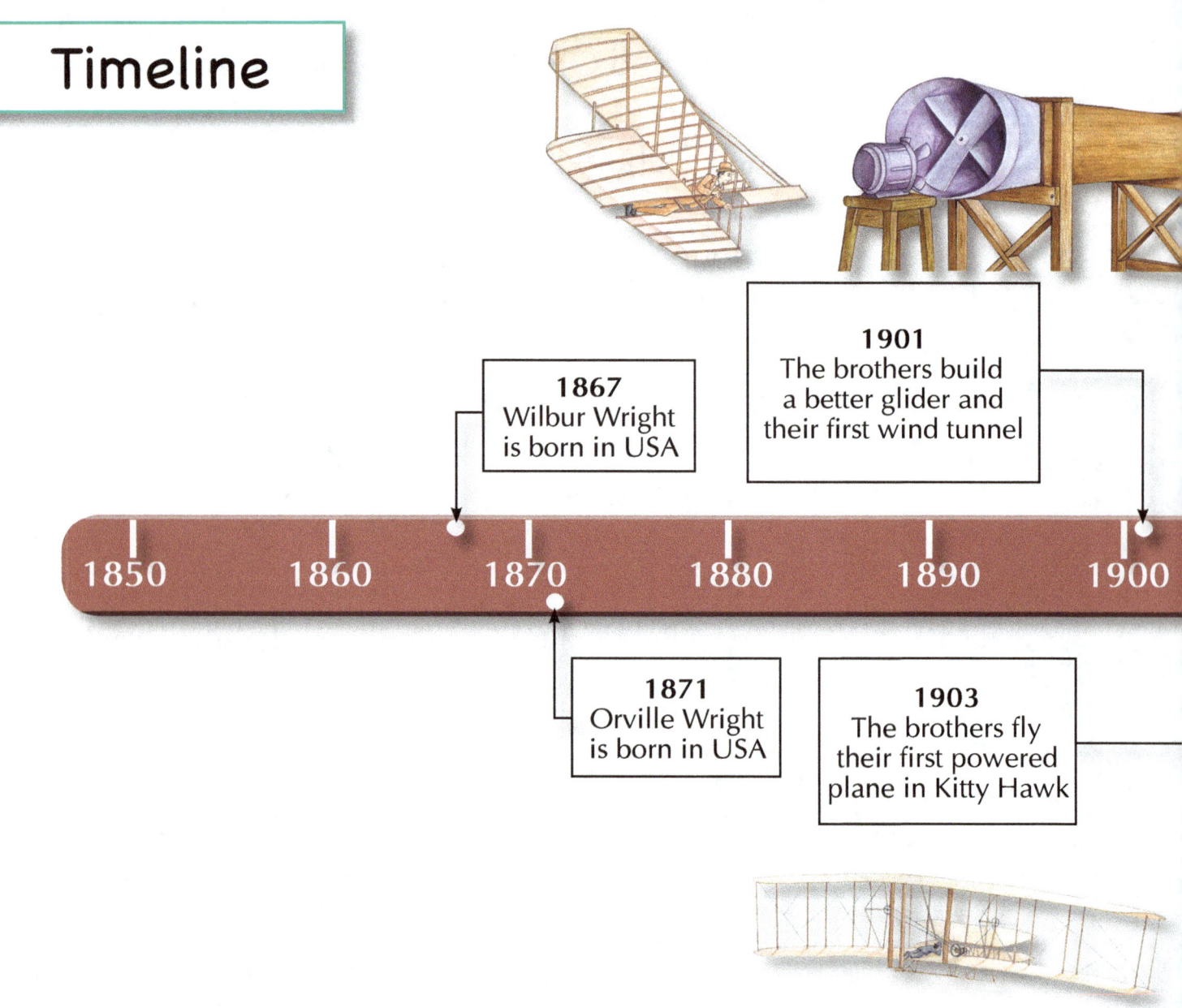

1867
Wilbur Wright
is born in USA

1901
The brothers build
a better glider and
their first wind tunnel

1871
Orville Wright
is born in USA

1903
The brothers fly
their first powered
plane in Kitty Hawk

1850   1860   1870   1880   1890   1900

Wilbur and Orville Wright's Lives and Works

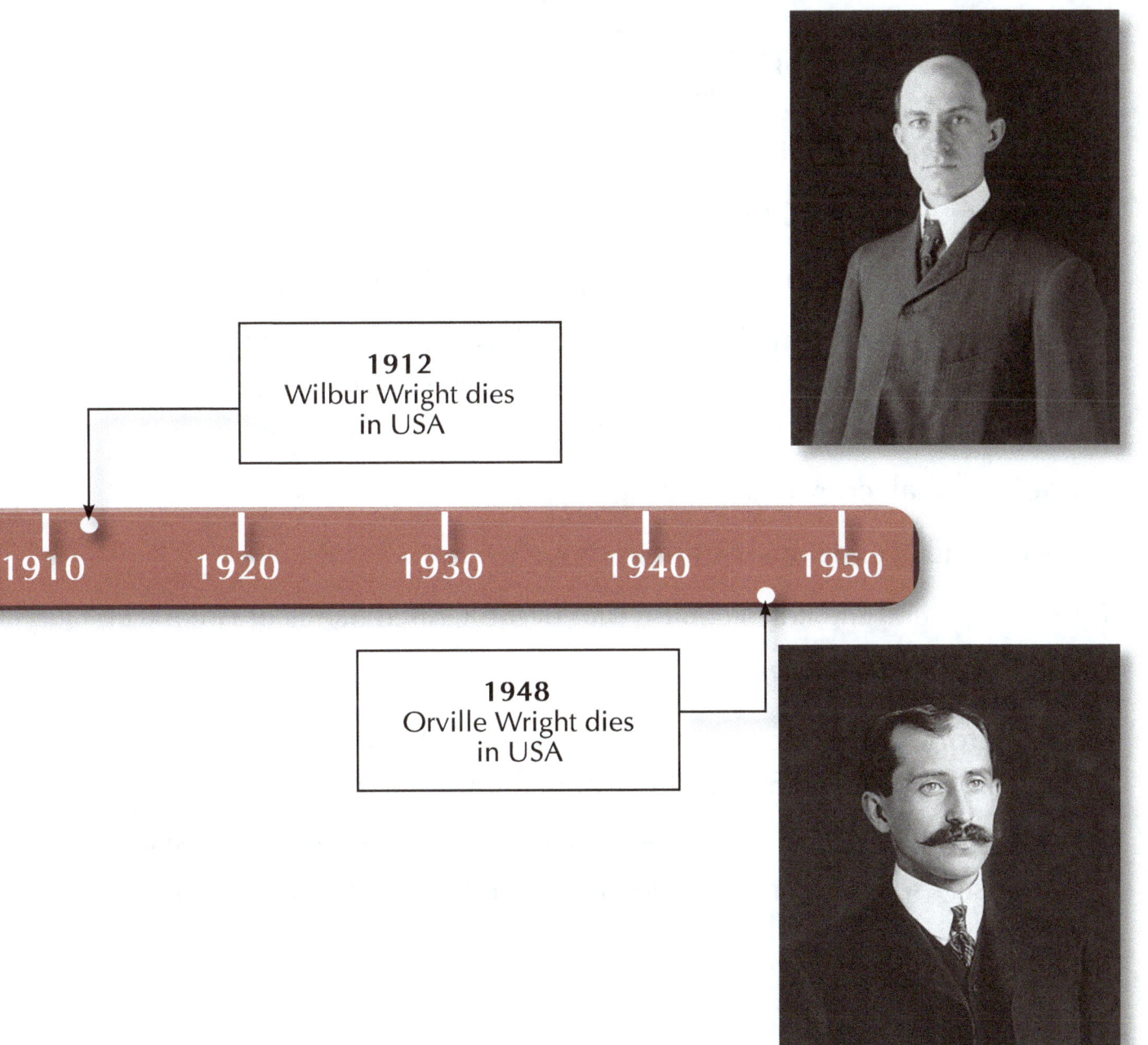

1912
Wilbur Wright dies
in USA

1948
Orville Wright dies
in USA

1910   1920   1930   1940   1950

Word Meanings

Glider: An airplane with no motor

Helicopter: A plane without wings that has a propeller on top

Indiana: A state in the north central part of the United States of America

Kitty Hawk, North Carolina: Kitty Hawk is a town in North Carolina. North Carolina is a state in the south-eastern part of the United States. The Wright Brothers flew their first plane in a field at Kitty Hawk.

Model: A small copy of something

Motor: A device that makes things move

Ohio: A state in the north central part of the United States of America

Steer: To make something go in a certain direction

Washington, D.C.: A city in the United States. Washington, D.C. is the capital of the United States. It is where the president lives.

Wind tunnel: A machine that can measure speed and direction of wind. Scientists use wind tunnels to learn how to build better airplanes.

Think, Talk and Write

Think About It

Think about how the Wright brothers learned to make an airplane.
Make a list of the things that helped the Wright brothers learn how to build an airplane.
Draw a picture of one of the things on your list.

Talk About It

Work with a partner.
Talk about why inventing the airplane was an important event.
Work together to make a list of your reasons.

Write About It

How is the airplane that the Wright brothers built like the planes of today?
How is it different?
What if you could write an email to the Wright Brothers?
Tell them about how their invention is alike and different from the airplanes of today.

What did you learn from Wright Brothers?

What are the five things that you will change after reading the Wright Brothers' story?

....

....

....

....

....

....

....

....

....

....

....

....

....

....

James Watt

James Watt invented the steam engine.
He also invented many other things.
Read on to discover what he invented.

Meet Tim and Tyra

Hi, I'm Tim.

Hi, I'm Tyra. We are going to travel back in time to visit James Watt. Let's meet him now.

James Watt was born on 19 January, 1736 in Greenock, **Scotland**.
Watt was a **scientist** and an **inventor**.

James Watt did not go to school like other children.
He was a weak child.
So, his mother taught him to read and draw at home.
His father taught him mathematics.
He also taught young James to use tools.

James Watt loved to work in his **workshop**.
He learned to work with different metals and wood.
He made many instruments.
He made many models of **pulleys** and **cranes**.

Once, James Watt was asked to repair an engine. It was an early type of steam engine. He found that it had many problems. It used too much fuel. It was not efficient.
Watt had an idea! He wanted to make a better steam engine.

Watt worked on his idea for several months.
Finally, he came up with a better steam engine.
His engine used less fuel. It was also more efficient.
It was used for pumping water out of **mines**.

In 1774, James Watt set up his own company in **England**. He made steam engines. He sold over 500 engines. Watt made a lot of money.

James Watt **invented** the flyball governor.
It helped his steam engines work well.
The flyball governor regulated the speed of the engine.

James Watt invented a copying machine.
He called it a press copier.
It made copies of documents.
It used ink mixed with gum.
He made and sold his press copiers.

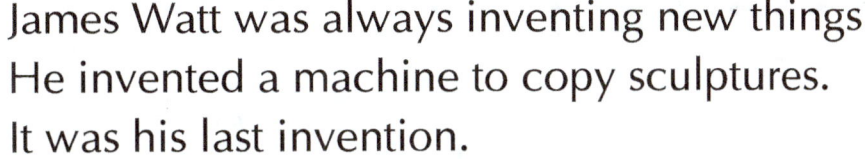

James Watt was always inventing new things.
He invented a machine to copy sculptures.
It was his last invention.

James Watt died on 25 August, 1819 in Staffordshire, England.

He was a great engineer.
You can visit his workshop.
It is in **London**! It has many of his drawings and inventions too.

Timeline

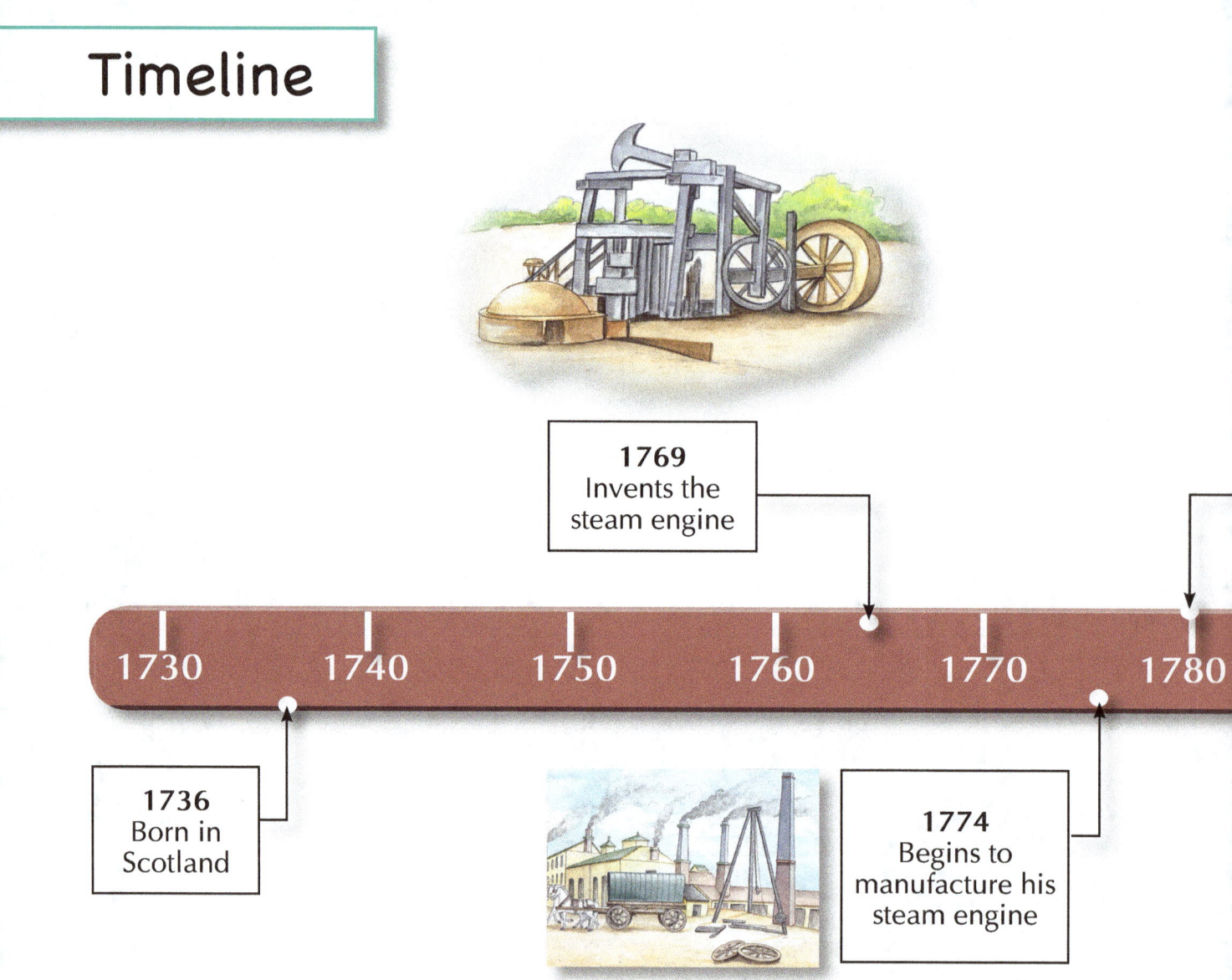

1769
Invents the
steam engine

1730　　1740　　1750　　1760　　1770　　1780

1736
Born in
Scotland

1774
Begins to
manufacture his
steam engine

James Watt's Life and Work

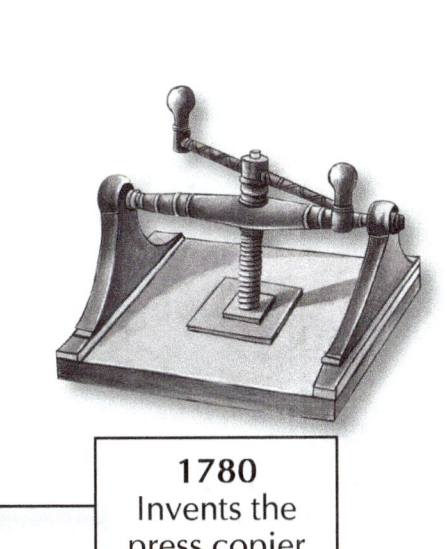

1780
Invents the
press copier

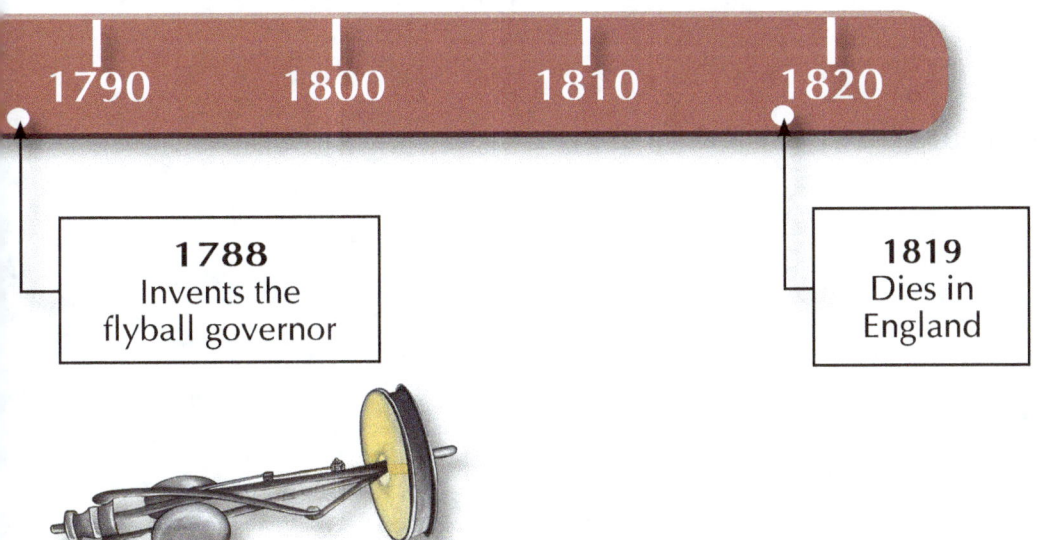

1790   1800   1810   1820

1788
Invents the
flyball governor

1819
Dies in
England

Word Meanings

Crane: A machine that can lift and move heavy objects

England: Part of the United Kingdom, a country in Europe

London: A city in England. London is the capital of the United Kingdom

Mine: To dig coal or another substances out of the ground

Pulley: A wheel with a groove along its edge to hold a rope or cable

Scotland: A constituent country of the United Kingdom in the northern part of Great Britain.

Workshop: A place to make new things

Think, Talk and Write

Think About It

James Watt invented many different things.
Which thing did you find the most interesting? Why?
Draw a picture showing the thing you found the most interesting.

Talk About It

How would you describe James Watt?
Tell a partner about him.
Tell your partner what he did.

Write About It

James Watt solved problems with his inventions.
What would you invent? Draw your invention.
Write three sentences explaining what problem it solves.

What did you learn from James Watt?

....

....

....

....

....

....

....

....

....

....

....

....

....

....

What are the five things that you will change after reading James Watt's story?

....

....

....

....

....

....

....

....

....

....

....

....

....

Work Space